Text copyright © 2025 Rennie Dyball
Cover art and interior illustrations copyright © 2025 Loyola Press

All rights reserved
Illustrator: Maine Diaz   Editor: Gary Jansen   Designer: Jill Arena

ISBN: 978-0-8294-5877-0
Library of Congress Control Number: 2024950304

Printed in China
24 25 26 27 28 29 30 31 32 33 DC 10 9 8 7 6 5 4 3 2 1

Fiona
AND THE PECULIAR PRAISE

by Rennie Dyball

illustrated by Maine Diaz

MY NAME IS FIONA

—that's short for Queen Fiona of Apartment 4C. My mom, my dad, and my sister, Lou, all live with me, and they are mostly fine people to have around.

EXCEPT FOR ONE PROBLEM.

The trouble started this morning, before the sun came up. I sat on Mom's head to wake her.

Mom said, "Too early, pretty kitty."

"PRETTY"?

That's a peculiar thing to call someone alerting you to breakfast time.

After eating, I went on my daily hallway prowl.
Soon I spotted an intruder. I pounced!
Then I scratched at the neighbor's welcome mat
until she answered the door.

"Eeeew, a mouse!" the neighbor shrieked.
"Would you please get it out of here, Lovely?"

UM, "LOVELY"?

How about "Great job once again, Fiona," since I'm always looking out for you scaredy-cats?

I scowled at the neighbor and carried the mouse —who did a magnificent job of playing dead—to the garbage chute. Then I whispered directions for him to sneak out of the building.

(DON'T TELL ANYONE, BUT I LET ALL THE MICE GO.)

Back in the apartment, it was time for a snooze in the big patch of sun.

"Getting your beauty sleep?" asked Dad.

"BEAUTY SLEEP"?!

I am resting my tired muscles after the morning hunt, thank you very much!

When I woke from my nap, I went to the bathroom in the silly sandbox rather than using my favorite spot behind the desk.

SEE?
I CAN BE CONSIDERATE.

"FIONA!!!"

Hmm . . . wonder what she's so upset about.

As the sun set, my people presented me with a new toy.
I raced back and forth across the carpet, attacking it.

"Aww, isn't she cute?" said Mom.

OH, FOR CRYING OUT LOUD, I AM NOT "CUTE"!

How could my family miss the show I was putting on right under their noses?

I AM FAST!

AND STRONG!

As Mom and Lou sat down for dinner,
Dad opened his laptop. I leapt onto the table and
plopped myself down on his keyboard.

"Is it dinnertime, Gorgeous?" Dad asked, laughing as he closed the computer.

"GORGEOUS"?! THAT'S IT.

I am OUT of patience now.
I've done amazing things today, but all anyone
can talk about is the way I look!

Oh, I can't take it anymore!

CAN'T... THESE... PEOPLE... SEE... THAT... I AM...

IF SHE CALLS ME ADORABLE,
I will swipe every fork, plate,
and spoon off this table.

"I love how smart she is!"

Lou exclaimed.

"Fiona is Mom's alarm clock every morning," Lou said.

"She catches the mice on our floor."

The whole room turned quiet. Mom and Dad smiled.

"You're right, Lou," said Mom. Dad nodded his head.

WELL, THIS IS QUITE
A TURN OF EVENTS.
I MEAN, LOU IS CORRECT.

I <u>AM</u> SMART.

MAYBE MY PEOPLE
ARE SMART, TOO.